A Fabulous Discovery

"You'll never guess what I found out today," Jessica cried, bouncing up and down on her toes. *"I found out who Mrs. Harrington really is!"*

Mrs. Wakefield and Elizabeth stared at Jessica. *"Who?"* they cried in unison.

Jessica pointed at the television set. *"There she is. There's Mrs. Harrington!"*

Elizabeth stared at the old black-and-white movie that was flickering on the screen. The face of the movie star that stared at her wasn't the thin, lined face of an old woman. It was the face of a beautiful young woman with high cheekbones and a dazzling smile.

Mrs. Wakefield gasped. *"So that's where I've seen her!"* she exclaimed.

"That's right!" Jessica crowed triumphantly. *"Old Mrs. Harrington is really Dolores Dufay, glamorous stage and screen star!"*

SWEET VALLEY TWINS

Jessica on Stage

Written by
Jamie Suzanne

Created by
FRANCINE PASCAL

A BANTAM SKYLARK BOOK®
NEW YORK · TORONTO · LONDON · SYDNEY · AUCKLAND

RL 4, 008-012

JESSICA ON STAGE

A Bantam Skylark Book / September 1989

ISBN 0-553-15747-7

Jessica
on Stage

One

◈

"Oh, no! What a disaster!" Jessica Wakefield cried one rainy Saturday afternoon. "Look what time it is!"

"It's two-fifteen," said Elizabeth, Jessica's identical twin. "So what?"

"I was supposed to bake cookies for the Unicorn meeting this afternoon, that's what," Jessica moaned. She ran her hands through her long blond hair. "I forgot, and now it's too late! The meeting's at three-thirty." She rolled her eyes dramatically and sank down into a chair with a sigh. "Lila Fowler will absolutely *kill* me! What am I going to do?"

Elizabeth tried to hold back a smile. Her twin was always exaggerating. She had a flair for being dramatic. Only a couple of weeks earlier, Jessica and Elizabeth had gone to the Sweet Valley Community Theater to see a play put on by a famous touring company. The next day, Jessica went to the library and took out a biography of Sarah Bernhardt, a famous actress. She read every single word of it, and now she was convinced that she was the next Sarah Bernhardt.

Although Elizabeth could understand her sister's love of the theater, she herself was not interested in acting. In fact, except for their long blond hair, their blue-green eyes, and the dimple in their left cheeks, they had hardly anything in common. Elizabeth, who was four minutes older than Jessica, was the more serious and responsible twin. She loved working on *The Sweet Valley Sixers*, the sixth-grade newspaper at Sweet Valley Middle School, and hoped to become a serious writer some day. She spent a lot of her free time reading, especially mysteries and horse stories. Horses were her favorite animals, and she took riding lessons once a week.

But Jessica was only interested in one animal—the mythical, magical unicorn. It was the symbol of the Unicorn Club, a group of girls who considered themselves to be the prettiest, most popular girls at school, and Jessica was honored to be a member. In fact, to show how special they were, every day they tried to wear something purple, the color of royalty. In addition to being one of the Unicorns, Jessica belonged to the Boosters, a cheerleading squad. And she was always interested in trying out for school plays. She loved being the center of attention. And right now was no exception.

"What am I going to do?" Jessica repeated loudly.

"Do about what?" Mrs. Wakefield asked, coming into the kitchen.

"Oh, Mom," Jessica exclaimed, jumping up. "You have to help me. I'm in very serious trouble!"

"What kind of trouble, Jessica?" Mrs. Wakefield asked. "What's the matter?" A worried crease crossed her brow.

Jessica wrung her hands and screwed up her face. "Something is terribly, terribly wrong! I need—"

"What she needs," Elizabeth interrupted quietly, "is a couple of dozen cookies."

Mrs. Wakefield sighed. "Jessica, I *wish* you'd stop exaggerating."

"But I'm not exaggerating!" Jessica wailed. "I promised Lila that I'd bring cookies to the Unicorn meeting this afternoon. I was supposed to bake them and it's too late for that. Will you drive me to the supermarket so I can buy some, Mom?"

"Why can't you walk?" Elizabeth asked.

"Because it's raining!" Jessica cried. "Please, Mom, I *have* to bring the cookies. It's my responsibility! You want me to meet my responsibilities, don't you?"

"Oh, all right, Jess," Mrs. Wakefield said, giving in. "But the next time you have to meet a

4

responsibility, would you try thinking of it more than five minutes ahead of time?"

Jessica nodded and quickly ran to the door. "We'd better hurry. Lila will never forgive me if I'm late for the meeting!"

It was still drizzling when Elizabeth, Jessica, and Mrs. Wakefield came out of the store. Jessica was skipping happily, carrying the two bags of chocolate mint cookies her mother had bought. The three of them climbed into the family's maroon van, then Mrs. Wakefield started the car and headed for the parking lot exit.

Just before she reached a stop sign, a brown dachshund darted out in front of them. Mrs. Wakefield jammed on the brakes to avoid hitting the dog, and they were bumped from the rear. The van rocked for an instant.

"Uh-oh," Elizabeth said.

"We've been hit!" Jessica screamed.

"Are you all right, girls?" Mrs. Wakefield asked. When they both nodded, she said, "I don't think it's too serious. We weren't going very quickly. The driver behind us must have been following too closely to stop."

She unfastened her seat belt and got out to inspect the damage. Elizabeth and Jessica followed.

There was only a tiny scratch in the heavy rubber crash guard on the bumper of the van, and the other car had a slight dent in the right front fender.

"Ooh, my *neck*," came a faint voice from behind them.

The other driver was sitting behind the wheel of her car. She was an elderly woman with white hair. Her thin, lined face was twisted with pain.

Mrs. Wakefield stepped up to the car window. "Are you hurt?" she inquired anxiously.

"What a *ridiculous* question!" the woman snapped. "Of *course* I'm hurt! My neck is badly injured and it's all your fault. You stopped right in front of me."

"But I had to stop," Mrs. Wakefield pointed out. "A dog ran out in front of me. If you'd been just a little further back, you would have been able to stop in time, too."

The woman winced. "So you're going to blame the whole thing on me!" she cried. She closed her eyes and slumped back in the seat.

Mrs. Wakefield opened the car door. "Perhaps it would be a good idea if we took you to the emergency room and let a doctor examine your neck."

"But, Mom," Jessica protested. "I have to get to the meeting!"

The woman's eyes flew open. "Yes, I think I should see a doctor." She climbed out of the car and handed Mrs. Wakefield her keys. "Just park my car over there," she instructed. "I'll have my insurance agent inspect it and call to let you know the cost of the damage."

"Mo-om," Jessica began, tugging frantically at her mother's arm. "The meeting—"

"Jessica and Elizabeth," Mrs. Wakefield said calmly, "would you please help this lady to the van? Mrs.—"

"Mrs. Harrington," the woman supplied. She

leaned on Jessica, closing her eyes weakly. "I should get to the emergency room right away," she said. "I'm sure I'm very badly hurt."

But after the emergency room doctor had examined Mrs. Harrington, they learned that she didn't have any serious injuries.

"She has some pain in her neck," he told Mrs. Wakefield, as they sat in the waiting room. "But the X ray shows absolutely no damage. I've advised her that the problem is a muscle strain. It's not at all serious, and she'll feel much better in a day or two."

"Oh, good," Jessica exclaimed, jumping up from her chair. She had been fidgeting anxiously for the last twenty minutes while they waited for the doctor's report. She was upset that the Unicorn meeting was starting without her. "That means we can go now, right, Mom?"

"In a minute, Jessica," Mrs. Wakefield said. She turned to the doctor. "Are you going to release Mrs. Harrington? Can we take her home?"

The doctor frowned. "I understand that she lives alone, and since she *is* sixty-five—"

Elizabeth looked at the doctor, surprised. That wasn't even as old as Grandmother Wakefield! The woman had seemed much older than that.

"—and because she's quite insistent about being looked after," the doctor continued, "I think it would be a good idea to keep her here for twenty-four hours. It's not absolutely necessary, but it can't hurt. We'll see that she gets home tomorrow afternoon."

Mrs. Wakefield nodded. "Well, then, I guess that's all for now." She stood up and shook his hand. "Thank you, doctor."

"Finally," Jessica said in a pouty voice, as they walked out of the emergency room. "The Unicorn meeting must be half over by now. Everybody will be furious with me."

"Well," Elizabeth said cheerfully, "at least Mrs. Harrington wasn't hurt. And there's barely even a scratch on her car. It could have been a whole lot worse, I guess."

Mrs. Wakefield nodded. "You know," she said, in a thoughtful voice, "Mrs. Harrington's face seemed so familiar. I'm certain that I've seen

9

her somewhere before. I just can't figure out where."

Jessica stuck out her lower lip. "Oh, Mom, that sounds just like a line from a movie. You've probably never seen her before in your life!" Flinging her blond hair over her shoulders, she dashed through the rain to the van.

"You're probably right, Sarah Bernhardt," Mrs. Wakefield said with a laugh.

Two

◇

It was still raining on Sunday morning. Jessica was curled up on the sofa in the family room studying acting—which meant watching old movies on television—while Elizabeth helped her mother clean up from breakfast.

When the dishes were done, Elizabeth wandered restlessly to the kitchen window and looked out at the steady drizzle. "I keep thinking about Mrs. Harrington," she said. "She must be so lonely. I wonder if she'd like some company."

"That's a wonderful idea, dear," Mrs. Wakefield said. "Why don't we both go see her?" She
paused. "You know, I still think I've seen her
before. I just can't figure out where."

"How about bringing some flowers to her?"
Elizabeth suggested. She gazed out the window
at the marigolds and daisies that were blooming
in the garden.

"I'm sure Mrs. Harrington would love them,"
Mrs. Wakefield agreed. "Do you suppose Jessica would like to go with us?"

"Go where?" Jessica asked, coming into the
kitchen. She went to the refrigerator and took
out a soda.

"To the hospital to visit Mrs. Harrington,"
Elizabeth replied.

Jessica made a face. "That old sourpuss? You
can count me out. Lila and the others were
pretty mad at me for being late with the cookies,
and it was all Mrs. Harrington's fault."

"Well, then, I guess Mom and I will go,"
Elizabeth said. She grabbed an umbrella from
the closet and went outside to pick some flowers.

Mrs. Harrington was propped up in bed, staring out the window at the cloudy sky. In spite of the fact that she was wearing an awkward neck brace, she looked rested and much less anxious than when they had brought her to the hospital the day before. Now, with her white hair pulled off her neck and piled high on her head, Elizabeth could see that she had a striking face, with high cheekbones, a firm jaw, and a fine sculptured nose. Elizabeth guessed that she had once been a very beautiful woman.

Mrs. Harrington's gray eyes brightened when she saw Elizabeth and her mother. Elizabeth handed her the bouquet of marigolds and daisies, which she had put into a pretty yellow vase.

"Are these for me?" Mrs. Harrington asked, sniffing the flowers. "How thoughtful of you." She gave Mrs. Wakefield an embarrassed smile. "Especially after the awful way I acted yesterday afternoon." She sighed. "I know I made a big fuss. I must have been quite a nuisance,

13

especially when your daughter was so anxious to get to her meeting."

Elizabeth was surprised. She didn't think that Mrs. Harrington had noticed Jessica's impatience.

Mrs. Wakefield sat down in the chair beside the bed and patted the woman's hand. "Well, it was a pretty traumatic event," she said consolingly. "I'm just glad that you weren't hurt seriously. And of course, I'm glad that there's no damage to either of the cars." She paused. "If you'd like, my husband and I will pick up your car and drop it off at your house."

"Would you?" Mrs. Harrington sighed gratefully. "I do apologize. I told my insurance agent over the phone that the accident was my fault. I don't take the car out very often anymore, and anyway, I'm not the best of drivers. I always depended on my husband to do the driving, and he's . . ." Her voice trailed off sadly, and she gazed past them, out the window, with a faraway look in her eyes.

Elizabeth waited for Mrs. Harrington to finish

what she was saying about her husband. But she didn't say another word.

"Will you have to wear the neck brace for very long?" she asked finally.

Mrs. Harrington pulled her gaze away from the window. "For a week or so," she replied. She sniffed the flowers again, and then handed them to Elizabeth, who put them on the bedside table. "Wearing this brace means that I won't be able to do any housework for the next few days. Of course," she added, "I don't suppose it matters very much whether the house is clean or not. I live alone. There's nobody to see whether the furniture is dusted or the carpet is vacuumed." She let out a long, sad sigh.

Elizabeth leaned forward, feeling a surge of compassion. Mrs. Harrington sounded so lonely. "Does your family live too far away to visit?" she asked sympathetically.

There was a long pause. "I don't have any family," Mrs. Harrington said at last, a note of self-pity creeping into her voice. "My husband, Richard, has been dead for eight years. We worked together, and both of us were very busy with our careers. We traveled a good deal, you see, and there just didn't seem to be any time in our lives for children." She paused again, her eyes sad and wistful. "I wish now that we'd had a family, but of course it's much too late to think about that."

Elizabeth was sorry that she had asked about Mrs. Harrington's family. Her question had only made the old woman feel worse. Quickly, she tried to change the subject to something more cheerful, but Mrs. Harrington had already turned her head away.

"I'm very tired," she said in a thin voice, leaning back on the pillow. "And my neck hurts terribly. I think I'd like to rest now, if you don't mind."

Mrs. Wakefield stood up. "Of course," she said. "If there's anything we can do to help when you get home, I hope you'll let us know."

"There's nothing *anybody* can do," Mrs. Harrington said sadly. She never turned to look at them as they left the room.

16

*   *   *

When Elizabeth and Mrs. Wakefield got home, Jessica ran into the kitchen to greet them. "You'll never guess what I found out today," she cried, bouncing up and down on her toes. "You'll never guess in a million years!"

"Hollywood called and offered you a contract for two movies?" Mrs. Wakefield guessed.

Jessica rolled her eyes. "Very funny, Mom." She grinned. "Actually, though, it does have to do with a famous star. So you're getting warm. Guess again."

"Johnny Buck called and asked you for a date?" Elizabeth tried. Johnny Buck was Jessica's favorite rock star.

Jessica flashed her twin an impatient look. But she was so excited about her discovery that she obviously couldn't be bothered with getting angry. "I found out who Mrs. Harrington *really* is!"

Elizabeth and her mother stared at Jessica. "You did?" Elizabeth said. "Well, tell us who she is!"

17

"Yes," Mrs. Wakefield said. "I've been trying to figure it out since yesterday."

"Come on," Jessica commanded, grabbing her mother's hand and pulling her toward the family room. "I'll do better than that. I'll show you!"

Laughing, Mrs. Wakefield let herself be pulled along, and Elizabeth trailed behind, shaking her head.

"There she is," Jessica cried, pointing to the television as they entered the room. "There's Mrs. Harrington!"

Elizabeth stared at the old black-and-white movie that was flickering on the screen. The face of the movie star that stared at her wasn't the thin, lined face of the old woman she had just left in the hospital. It was the joyful, expressive face of a beautiful young woman—a woman with high cheekbones, a firm jaw, a fine nose, and a very dazzling smile.

Mrs. Wakefield gasped. "So that's where I've seen her!" she exclaimed. "In the movies! No wonder I had the feeling I knew her well! *Winds of Eden* used to be my favorite movie."

"That's right!" Jessica crowed triumphantly. "Old Mrs. Harrington is really Dolores Dufay, glamorous stage and screen star!"

Three

"I just can't believe it," Jessica said ecstatically. The twins were sitting at the kitchen table with their mother, sipping hot chocolate and munching on cookies. "A famous movie star, right here in Sweet Valley."

Mrs. Wakefield poured the girls another cup of hot chocolate and took the pan to the sink. "But Dolores Dufay wasn't only famous and beautiful," she said, sitting down again. "She was also a very fine actress. She and her husband, Richard Harrington, were a husband-and-wife acting team back in the forties and fifties. As I remember, they started out in New York, on Broadway. Then later they were cast as the romantic leads in a couple of big Hollywood movies. They shot up to stardom in a hurry, but they were known best for the quality of their work." She picked up a cookie and took a bite. "In fact, I think Richard Harrington was even nominated for an Academy Award once."

Jessica's mouth dropped open. "Wow! An Academy Award!" she exclaimed.

Mrs. Wakefield nodded. "As they got older, they went on to play character roles. But whatever they did, their work was always very fine."

"I can't wait to see one of her newer movies," Jessica said. "What has she starred in recently?"

Mrs. Wakefield shook her head. "You know, that's the odd thing," she said. "I can't remember seeing her in anything in the past several years. She's sort of dropped out of sight."

"But if Mrs. Harrington was such a wonderful actress, why isn't she still acting?" Elizabeth wondered.

"Maybe she's getting too old," Jessica suggested.

Mrs. Wakefield smiled. "No, dear. I don't think one is ever too old to act." She leaned forward and tapped the tip of Jessica's nose with a playful gesture. "Or too young to start."

Jessica didn't say anything. She turned her cup of hot chocolate around and around in her hands and gazed out the window with a distant look in her eyes.

Elizabeth stared at her sister. When Jessica got that look, it usually meant she was hatching a plan. Elizabeth was fiercely loyal to her twin and always stood up for her, no matter what. But even she had to admit that Jessica frequently came up with some farfetched schemes. What was it this time? And was the famous Dolores Dufay part of her plan?

The next morning when the twins got to school, Elizabeth waited for Jessica to tell all her friends—especially the Unicorns— about her fabulous discovery. She was amazed when Jessica didn't say a single word about the old lady or the beautiful film star.

Instead, Jessica just listened while everyone crowded around Amy Sutton and Belinda Layton, two of Elizabeth's good friends.

"Elizabeth," Amy cried out excitedly, "wait until you see the kitten Belinda and I found this weekend. It's the cutest thing!"

"It's black and white, and we found it in the vacant lot near the Little League field," Belinda continued.

Jessica wrinkled up her nose. "What's so great about a stray kitten?" she asked. "It's probably real scrawny and has fleas all over it."

"It does *not* have fleas," Belinda protested. "It's very clean." She paused. "And it *is* thin, but that's because it hasn't had much to eat in a while."

"We have a problem, though," Amy said. "Neither of us can take the kitten home. My mom's allergic to cats, and Belinda's mom doesn't want to have a kitten around their new baby. So the kitty's living under some old boards by the

23

fence, and it's really scared. We've been trying to get it to eat, but it's afraid to come close to us."

"What you need," Ken Matthews said, "is some liver."

"Liver, yuck!" Jessica shouted.

"Why liver?" Amy asked Ken.

Ken had recently gotten a dog and he knew a lot about taking care of animals. "Cats love liver," he explained.

"Well, we may as well try it," Belinda said. "Let's get some liver at Sweet Valley Super Market and take it over to the vacant lot after school."

"OK, if we each chip in twenty cents," Amy calculated, "we'll probably have enough money." She turned to Elizabeth. "Can you come with us, Elizabeth? You have to see this kitty."

Elizabeth was about to say yes when Jessica stopped her.

"Elizabeth can't go anywhere after school today," she told the others firmly.

Elizabeth stared at Jessica suspiciously. "I can't?" If Jessica's grand scheme involved Dolores Dufay, she was going to say no. "Why can't I?"

"Because," Jessica said mysteriously, "you and I have an important errand to do."

The others were conferring in excited voices about the kitten, and Elizabeth moved closer to her twin.

"Jessica, if you're planning to use that poor Mrs. Harrington to—"

"*Use* Mrs. Harrington?" Jessica interrupted her. She looked hurt. "Who said anything about *using* her? I was thinking of doing something nice for her, that's all. I'd really like to get to know her. Wouldn't you?" She gave Elizabeth a wide-eyed, innocent look.

"Do something nice for her?" Elizabeth asked. That didn't sound like Jessica. "What sort of thing?"

"Something like taking her some special tea to cheer her up. We could stop by that gourmet food store on Canyon Avenue on our way to her house. We have our allowance money."

"But we don't know where Mrs. Harrington lives," Elizabeth objected.

25

"Yes, we do," Jessica replied calmly. "I got her address from Mom. She and Dad took Mrs. Harrington's car back, remember? Actually, she lives less than a mile away. We can walk there."

"You're *sure* that all you want to do is get to know her?" Elizabeth asked.

"Yes, Lizzie, I promise. I just want to hear about her adventures in Hollywood. That's all."

Elizabeth sighed. She couldn't help but think that Jessica had some other motive for wanting to visit the famous actress. But she had to admit that she was curious about Mrs. Harrington's former life in Hollywood, too. And it *would* be a nice gesture to take her some tea.

"Are you *sure* this is the right street?" Jessica asked uncertainly, looking at the houses on both sides of the road as she and Elizabeth walked along. "It doesn't look at all the way I thought it would." She had expected to see big, fancy houses surrounded by luxurious, landscaped lawns, with sleek, expensive sports cars parked outside. What she saw instead were two neat rows of perfectly ordinary houses—small, modest homes with children playing in the front yards—and perfectly ordinary cars parked in the driveways.

"Maybe I copied down the wrong address," Jessica said, almost hoping she had.

"Maybe," Elizabeth said, switching the bag of teas from one hand to the other. "But we're almost there. Let's just check to be sure."

"There it is," Jessica said, pointing to a small green house at the end of the block.

The house was even smaller than the others on the street, and not so well kept up. The lawn needed mowing, the bushes looked as if they hadn't been trimmed in months, and a front window was cracked.

Elizabeth rang the doorbell while Jessica stood behind her, checking her school bag to be sure that her autograph book was still there. Jessica hadn't told her sister she was bringing it, but she wasn't about to miss this wonderful chance of getting a real live movie star to sign it. She couldn't wait to see Lila Fowler's and Ellen

Riteman's faces when she told them about meeting Dolores Dufay and showed them her autograph.

Mrs. Harrington finally opened the door, interrupting Jessica's daydream. She didn't look at all pleased to see them. And she certainly didn't look like a famous movie star. In fact, Jessica thought, she looked like a tired old woman who had spent most of the afternoon crying. Her eyes were red and puffy, and the worry lines between her eyes looked deeper than Jessica remembered. The brace she wore around her neck made her movements stiff and awkward.

"Yes, of course I remember you, Elizabeth," Mrs. Harrington was saying. "But I'm not at all ready for guests today. Could you come back another time?"

"But we brought you something," Jessica said, stepping forward. She put on her brightest smile. "Won't you let us come in, just for a minute? We promise not to stay too long."

"But I don't think—" Mrs. Harrington began.

"Please?" Jessica begged.

Mrs. Harrington looked down at her. "Well," she said slowly, "since you've walked all the way here, I don't suppose it would hurt if you . . ." She opened the door reluctantly. "Come on in, but just for a minute."

Eagerly, Jessica stepped through the door. Once inside, she couldn't help gasping out loud. Mrs. Harrington's house was a horrible mess! The furniture was turned upside down. Drawers were pulled out of cabinets and lamps lay on the floor. Books and newspapers were scattered everywhere, and clothes lay in untidy heaps.

Behind Jessica, Elizabeth gasped, too. "What in the world *happened*?" she cried.

Mrs. Harrington heaved a deep sigh. "While I was in the hospital, somebody broke in and robbed my house." She pointed at the mess. "This is what they left. I just haven't had the energy to clean it up yet."

29

Four

◇

"It's just *terrible*," Jessica said sympathetically, looking around the kitchen. Drawers were pulled out and chairs were overturned. There was a pile of broken dishes in the middle of the floor. "You must feel awful."

Mrs. Harrington was putting on a kettle of water for tea. She turned, her shoulders slumping.

"Yes," she said. She turned one of the chairs right-side-up and sat down in it. "It was a terrible shock to come in and see things this way."

"Have you called the police?" Elizabeth asked, picking up a chair and righting it.

Mrs. Harrington nodded. "They've already been here. They took fingerprints, and they've asked me for a list of missing items. But aside from some antique jewelry that belonged to my husband's mother, I'm not even sure what's been taken." She glanced around, dismayed. "With this brace on my neck, it will probably take me weeks just to put everything back where it belongs. And I can't tell what's missing until everything is in its proper place." She looked as if she might start crying.

Jessica reached for a broom that was standing beside the back door and began to sweep up the broken dishes. Her autograph book was still in her bag, but under the circumstances, she didn't feel she could ask Mrs. Harrington to sign it.

Mrs. Harrington reached for a tissue. "You don't have to do that, Jessica," she said, blowing her nose.

"But I want to," Jessica protested. She threw the broken dishes into the wastebasket. It didn't matter whether Mrs. Harrington was a famous actress or an ordinary person. She still needed help.

Elizabeth threw her sister a surprised but pleased look. "Jessica's right," she said. "We'll be glad to help you put your house back in order."

The kettle began to whistle and Jessica poured the boiling water into the teapot, which held some of the cranberry tea they had brought. While the tea brewed, the girls worked in the kitchen, sweeping and cleaning and putting things back as Mrs. Harrington directed them. They stopped for a cup of the sweet, steaming tea, and then they went into the living room to clean up there.

"It's hard to know where to begin," Mrs. Harrington said, glancing around. She sounded as if she were ready to give up. "It's such a mess. And I'm so tired."

"Why don't I take this corner," Jessica suggested, "and Elizabeth can do the other corner. And you can just sit on the sofa and tell us what to do."

The twins worked for a while and Mrs. Harrington rested. Jessica sneaked a look at her. Sitting on the sofa, her face lined with weariness, obviously uncomfortable in her brace, Mrs. Harrington didn't look anything like the actress in *Winds of Eden*.

Jessica was cleaning under a table when she spotted a large framed picture turned on its face. Curiously, she picked it up and dusted it off. It was a portrait of Dolores Dufay at her most beautiful. She was wearing a sparkling evening gown and had a feather boa around her neck. Beside her knelt a handsome man with dark hair and piercing eyes.

Jessica whirled around, holding up the picture. "You *are* Dolores Dufay!" she cried excitedly. "Elizabeth, we were right!"

For a moment, Mrs. Harrington stared at Jessica. Then her eyes suddenly filled with tears and she got up from the sofa and rushed into the kitchen.

"Now you've done it, Jessica," Elizabeth said.

Jessica was filled with remorse. She hurried after Mrs. Harrington.

"I'm sorry, Mrs. Harrington," she said. "I didn't mean to upset you. I was just so excited that . . . well, I just didn't think, that's all."

Mrs. Harrington was sitting at the table, wiping her eyes. "That's all right, Jessica," she said sadly. "I probably overreacted. It's just that it's so hard to be reminded about what's in the past."

Elizabeth came into the kitchen and poured them all another cup of tea.

"Years ago, my husband and I were a famous acting team. And a successful one, too," Mrs. Harrington added. "We did very well." She made a sweeping gesture. "But as you can see, I don't have much now."

Jessica chewed on the corner of her lip. "But nobody knows that," she said. "If people found out who you were, they might think you had lots of jewelry."

Mrs. Harrington nodded. "I've always been afraid of that. People don't realize that not all movie stars make a mountain of money. They think that just because you were in the movies, you ought to be rich."

Jessica felt her face going red. It was exactly what she had thought. "Why did you stop acting?" she asked, hurriedly changing the subject.

Mrs. Harrington sipped her tea. "My husband and I did everything together. But he was by far the better performer, and I never really felt like an actress in my own right. *Winds of Eden* was our best film. After he died, eight years ago, that was the end of the team. And the end of my acting career. I haven't acted since then."

Mrs. Harrington stood up as if to indicate the end of their visit. "Thank you for coming, girls. And for the tea. It was very kind of you."

Jessica considered taking out her autograph book. But for some reason, she couldn't. It wouldn't be right. She said, instead, "We'd like to come back tomorrow and help clean up some more, if it's all right with you."

Mrs. Harrington looked surprised. Elizabeth looked even more surprised.

"Are you sure that you want to help?" Mrs. Harrington asked. "There's a great deal to do, I'm afraid."

"Jessica's right. We really want to help," Elizabeth said.

"Then please do come," Mrs. Harrington replied. "I'd love to have you." For the first time since they had met, she smiled, and Jessica could see a trace of the famous Dufay smile.

The following three afternoons, Jessica and Elizabeth went back to Mrs. Harrington's house after school to help out. They swept and dusted and put things back into the proper drawers and closets. And as they worked, they talked. Sometimes Jessica could get Mrs. Harrington to talk about her husband, Richard, whom she had clearly adored. And sometimes she would talk, just a little bit, about her feelings about acting. She was delighted to hear about Jessica's interest in acting, but she wouldn't answer any of her questions about Hollywood or her glamorous past. It all seemed as if it were a million years ago, she said. It was clear to the twins that when Richard Harrington died, a big part of Dolores Dufay's life ended, too. She had very few friends and she rarely went out anymore. Jessica just had to figure out some way to help her.

"You know, Jess," Elizabeth said on Wednesday evening, as they were walking home, "I think Mrs. Harrington really likes you."

"Good. I like her, too. I mean, she's a neat person, in addition to being a famous actress."

"I have to admit," Elizabeth confessed, "that I didn't trust your motives when you first wanted to visit her. I figured that you were after her autograph or something like that."

Jessica felt herself blushing. "You did?" she asked, with a little giggle. "Well, I guess I fooled you, huh?"

On Friday after school, Elizabeth went with Amy and Belinda to see their kitten while Jessica went alone to visit Mrs. Harrington.

Late in the afternoon, Elizabeth came home and found her mother in the family room leafing through a pile of design magazines.

Elizabeth sat down on the sofa, thinking about the best way to ask her mother the question she'd been turning over in her mind all day. Finally she just blurted it out.

"Mom," she said, "could we get a cat?"

"I never knew you wanted a cat, honey," Mrs. Wakefield said, glancing up from her magazine.

"Well, this is a special cat," Elizabeth explained. "She's almost all black except for the white on her two front paws, a little spot under her neck, and the tip of her tail."

"She sounds like a very pretty cat," Mrs. Wakefield said. She came over and sat down beside Elizabeth. "What makes her so special?"

"She's been living in the vacant lot beside the Little League field," Elizabeth replied. "Amy and Belinda found her, and they've been feeding her because she's so thin. She's very cute, Mom. And she needs a home."

"But if Amy found her, why can't Amy give her a home?"

"She'd love to, but her mom's allergic to cats."

"Well, then, what about Belinda?"

"Belinda's mom doesn't think it's a good idea, because of her new baby brother. And Ken can't because he's got a dog." Elizabeth looked pleadingly at her mother. "Please, Mom? I'll take care of her."

Mrs. Wakefield thought for a moment. "Well, I like cats. And having one around might be nice, as long as you'll take full responsibility."

"I will," Elizabeth promised. She jumped up and threw her arms around her mother. "Thank you, Mom! Tomorrow afternoon, after Belinda's Little League game, I'll bring the kitty home."

"OK, dear. Just remember, you'll need to get her some food and a litter box. And we'll have to take her to the vet to make sure she's in good health. I'm counting on you, Elizabeth. Maybe Jessica will help you out, too. By the way," Mrs. Wakefield said, glancing at the clock, "do you know where she is? It's almost time for dinner."

"She's probably on her way back from Mrs. Harrington's," Elizabeth said. "She went over there after school today."

Just then, Jessica came hurrying in. "Lizzie, I need to talk to you," she said breathlessly. "Right now!"

"What's wrong? What is it, Jess?"

"We've got to do something!" Jessica exclaimed. "Mrs. Harrington is practically heartbroken!"

"But I thought she was feeling so much better," Elizabeth said.

"She was—until she discovered that her scrapbook is missing. The thieves must have taken it."

"Her scrapbook?"

Jessica nodded. "I finally got her to talk about her acting career. She was even going to show me her scrapbook. But when she looked for it, it was gone. I think she feels worse about losing that, with all its clippings and pictures, than she feels about the jewelry."

Elizabeth could understand Mrs. Harrington's

feelings. "But I don't see what we can do," she said.

"We've got to find it for her!" Jessica cried. "Tomorrow morning, we'll go to the police station and talk to Officer Carey. Remember him? He's the policeman who came to our homeroom last month and gave that talk on safety. Maybe he'll have some ideas about where we can start searching."

"You know, Jessica," Elizabeth said thoughtfully, "for once you've come up with a good scheme that's not going to get us both in trouble. I'll do anything I can to help you look for Mrs. Harrington's scrapbook."

Five

◇

Officer Carey looked up from the papers on his desk. "So you want to help Mrs. Harrington," he stated. He reached for a file and began to thumb through it. "A few pieces of jewelry, pictures, books, scrapbook—not much of value was taken, I see."

"But her scrapbook is valuable," Jessica protested. She leaned forward. "It's the record of her entire acting career! We *have* to find it!"

Officer Carey nodded sympathetically. "I'm sure it's valuable to her," he said. "But it's worthless to a thief. In a burglary like this, the robber usually sells what he can and throws away the rest." He shrugged. "An old scrapbook—who knows where it ended up?"

"How about a secondhand store?" Elizabeth asked. "Or an antique shop?"

"You can try," the policeman said with a doubtful look. "But if you ask me, you girls are wasting your time."

Jessica stood up, feeling determined. "We're going to try," she said. "We have to help Mrs. Harrington."

The twins spent the morning searching every secondhand store and antique shop in Sweet Valley, talking to the owners and covering every inch of their stores. They even went to a local art gallery that often displayed old photos, but the owner hadn't seen any scrapbooks of that nature. Nobody had seen the book, and by afternoon, the girls were forced to admit that the scrapbook wasn't in any of the Sweet Valley shops.

On the way home, they stopped at the supermarket so Elizabeth could buy some cat food. As they walked out of the market, Elizabeth said, "I'm really sorry we didn't find the scrapbook, Jess. But we gave it a good try. I'll bet that the thief has probably thrown it away by now."

"I just don't believe that," Jessica said, shaking her head stubbornly. "I think it'll turn up *somewhere*. We have to keep looking, that's all. We have to think of some other places to look."

"Well," Elizabeth said, looking at her watch, "I can't search anymore this afternoon. I promised Amy and Belinda that we'd get the kitten and take her to our house. Want to come along?"

Jessica shook her head. "No, I don't think so."

Elizabeth said goodbye and headed off in the direction of the Little League field. The game was just over, and she threaded her way through the crowd to the Rangers' bench to find Belinda.

"How was the game?" she asked.

Belinda rubbed her shoulder. "It was close," she said. "But we won."

"You should have seen Belinda pitch!" Amy

44

exclaimed admiringly. "She was the star of the game!"

"Are you guys ready to go get the kitten?" Belinda asked, changing the subject. She looked a little sad. "I wish my mom would let *me* take her home."

"So do I," Amy said. "But I'm glad that Elizabeth's mom will let her keep it."

"Any time you want to come and play with her, you can," Elizabeth offered.

Belinda's face lit up. "Let's go find her," she said eagerly, setting out toward the vacant lot. The others followed.

The kitten was obviously anxious to see them. She pricked her ears forward, licked her whiskers, and stared with her big green eyes, as if expecting some food. Elizabeth picked her up and cuddled her, listening to her deep, rich purr. "Come on," she said happily. "You're coming home with me."

"She needs a name," Amy said, as they headed for the Wakefields' house.

"I have a great idea," Elizabeth announced.

"Let's all suggest names for her, and then pick the best one."

"That sounds good," Belinda agreed. She looked at the kitten snuggled into the crook of Elizabeth's arm. "With her black-and-white coat, maybe we should call her Patches."

As the girls walked home, they thought of several other names— Cuddles, Miss Kitty, Sweetie Pie.

When they reached the Wakefields', Elizabeth fed the kitten and gave her a small bowl of milk. The kitten gulped it up quickly, and licked all the drops off her chin. Then she darted from room to room, exploring the house. She couldn't jump very high yet, but she managed to jump up on a dining room chair and then onto the table, where she upset a bowl of nuts. After that, she ran into the family room and jumped into Mrs. Wake-field's knitting basket, jumbling all the balls of yarn.

Elizabeth, Belinda, and Amy followed after her, putting things back where they belonged.

"This cat," Amy observed as she picked up

some papers the kitten had scattered, "is a real mischief-maker." She grinned. "Maybe it's a good thing that my mom is allergic!"

"Why, Amy, that's it!" Elizabeth cried. "Mischief! That's a perfect name for the kitten."

Amy and Belinda agreed that it was definitely the right name, but before they could even try the name out, the kitten was sound asleep on the sofa, her tail curled over her nose.

Later that afternoon, Elizabeth fed Mischief another bowl of milk while Jessica sat at the kitchen table leafing through the Sweet Valley phone book. She wanted to make sure they hadn't overlooked any place where they might search for Mrs. Harrington's missing scrapbook.

"You know, Elizabeth," she said, "maybe we're taking the wrong approach."

Elizabeth took an apple from the refrigerator and sat down at the table. "The wrong approach to what?" she asked.

"To Mrs. Harrington's problem," Jessica said. "But we tried every place we could think of this morning," Elizabeth replied. "And we didn't find the scrapbook anywhere." She glanced at the phone book. "You haven't found any other place for us to look, have you?"

Jessica slammed the phone book shut. "No," she said glumly. "But maybe we ought to stop thinking about Mrs. Harrington's scrapbook for the moment. Maybe we ought to think about ways to cheer her up, instead."

Elizabeth tilted her head, thinking. "Yes, we could try that," she said. "Have you got any ideas?"

"That's just the trouble," Jessica replied dejectedly. "I've thought of lots of things, but there's always a reason why they wouldn't work." She began to tick ideas off on her fingers. "We could take her to the theater, but she doesn't like to go out at night and it may just make her feel sorry for herself. We could introduce her to other older people, but we don't know any. We could help her find a hobby, but she doesn't like to sew or cook or do crossword puzzles." She sighed.

Elizabeth nodded. "I see what you mean, Jess. It sounds like an almost unsolvable problem."

"What kind of problem?" Steven Wakefield demanded, coming into the kitchen and heading for the refrigerator. "*No* problem is too big for Steven the Great. What'll you give me to solve it?"

Steven was fourteen, two years older than the twins, and he had the idea that he was superior to them in every way. It was an attitude that infuriated Jessica. As far as she was concerned, her brother was an absolute pain.

She stuck out her tongue at him. "Steven the Great? Don't make me laugh. Don't you mean Steven the Creep?"

"Maybe we'd better tell him about our problem, Jess. You never know. He might just come up with an idea."

"I doubt it!" Jessica scoffed.

Steven removed a plate of sliced turkey, a loaf of bread, a head of lettuce, and a jar of mayonnaise from the refrigerator.

"The problem," Elizabeth explained, "is that

we have this older friend who lives all alone. She needs something to amuse her and keep her busy.''

Steven quickly slapped together a turkey sandwich, then took a big bite and said, with his mouth full, ''Well, that's simple. Get her a dog.''

Jessica gagged. ''Yuck! I hate dogs!''

''But your friend might like them. And look at it this way,'' Steven said confidentially, licking some mayonnaise off of his thumb, ''a dog will not only keep her company, but he'll protect her. With a dog, she'll never have to worry about somebody breaking into her house.''

Jessica hated to admit that her brother had even an ounce of brains, but in this case, his idea wasn't so bad.

''She'd have to take a dog for walks,'' she said to Elizabeth. ''Which means she'd have to go out and get some exercise. And if the dog was friendly, it might be a way for her to meet people.'' She frowned at Steven. ''But where would we get a dog? We don't have enough money to buy one.''

"Boy, is this your lucky day," Steven said. He took another enormous bite of his sandwich. "It just so happens that my friend Joe Oppenheimer has some German shepherd puppies to give away. All you have to do is go over there tomorrow and pick one out."

Jessica turned to Elizabeth. "What do you think, Lizzie?" she asked eagerly.

"Well, actually, I'm not sure that Mrs. Harrington—"

But Jessica didn't let her finish. "I know!" she exclaimed. "We could ask Ken to go over to Joe Oppenheimer's with us tomorrow and help us pick out a puppy. He knows all about dogs."

"But don't you think we should ask—" Elizabeth tried again.

Jessica jumped up. "Steven, I hate to say this. But every once in a while—maybe once in a million years—you come up with a good idea. Thanks."

Steven took a quart of milk out of the refrigerator and filled a tall glass. Then he piled a plate high with chocolate cookies and headed for the door. "I told you. Just call me Steven the Great," he said smugly.

"If you keep on eating like that," Jessica taunted, "we'll have to call you Steven the Huge."

Six

◇

"That's him," Jessica said, pointing to a large, energetic puppy. "That's the one for Mrs. Harrington."

"But I think this one would be better," Ken said, pointing to a smaller, quieter dog. "It seems to have a better disposition."

"But this one has more energy," Jessica objected. She turned to Elizabeth. "Don't you think this is the right one, Lizzie?"

Elizabeth shrugged. "If that's the one you want, Jess." She really didn't think that Mrs.

Harrington would like any of the puppies. They were all yapping and chasing one another around.

"Good." Jessica nodded with satisfaction. "That's the one we'll take."

Joe Oppenheimer picked up the puppy and handed it to Jessica. But she gave a little shriek and backed away.

"I'm not carrying it!" she said. "It'll slobber all over my blouse. Elizabeth, you carry it. You like dogs."

Elizabeth laughed. "You don't have to carry him, Jess. We'll put a leash on him."

The girls thanked Joe and said goodbye to Ken at the corner. Then they headed for Mrs. Harrington's house.

When they got there, Jessica knocked on the door while Elizabeth stood beside her, holding the leash. The puppy wrapped the leash around Elizabeth's ankles a couple of times and then looked up at her with a bewildered look, as if he were wondering why he couldn't move. Elizabeth laughed and picked him up, cradling him in her arms.

"Why, hello, Jessica!" Mrs. Harrington exclaimed as she opened the door. "And Elizabeth, too. I wasn't expecting you today. What a wonderful surprise!"

"And we've brought you another surprise," Jessica said. "A dog."

"A dog? For me?"

Elizabeth didn't think that Mrs. Harrington was exactly overjoyed. She stepped forward and put the puppy on the floor. But before she could get his leash unfastened, he took off like a shot, tearing through the house.

"Come back here!" Mrs. Harrington cried.

"Puppy, come back!" Jessica shouted. She turned to Elizabeth. "Catch him, Lizzie."

Elizabeth chased the puppy. He ran into the living room, trailing his leash and yelping at the top of his puppy lungs. He jumped up on the sofa, scattering cushions right and left.

"Catch him, Elizabeth!" Jessica urged. "Hurry! He's making a terrible mess!"

"Is he trained?" Mrs. Harrington asked anxiously.

"I don't know," Elizabeth replied, out of breath. She grabbed for the leash and missed. The puppy jumped off the sofa, just missing a lamp. "I doubt it."

The next moment, they knew for sure. The puppy was *not* trained.

"Well," Jessica said as she watched Elizabeth clean up the puddle with a handful of paper towels, "at least he didn't get the carpet all wet." Out on the porch, the puppy gave several indignant yelps. He didn't like being tied to the porch railing.

"Thank *heavens* he didn't soil my carpet," Mrs. Harrington said. She folded her arms. "Jessica and Elizabeth, I am sorry to tell you this, but a puppy is just too much work for an old woman like me. I can't look after him with my injured neck. As you can see, he'd create a terrible mess. And anyway, he'd cost too much to feed. He may be a small puppy now, but he's going to grow up to be a very large dog. Thank you for your thoughtfulness, but I just can't keep him."

Elizabeth wasn't at all surprised at the way things had turned out.

Jessica sighed. "Do you think you can take the puppy back to Joe's, Elizabeth? I'm going to stay and help Mrs. Harrington straighten things up."

Elizabeth felt very cross. She started to say that it would only take a minute to right the kitchen chair and straighten the lamp and put the cushions back on the sofa. This whole thing had been Jessica's idea in the first place. But she decided not to say anything in front of Mrs. Harrington. She apologized, said goodbye, and let the puppy drag her down the street.

"Would you like a cup of tea?" Mrs. Harrington asked, when Jessica had finished straightening things up. "I was just sitting down to one myself."

"That would be nice," Jessica said. She saw the newspaper spread out on the kitchen table. "Did we interrupt your reading?"

Mrs. Harrington sighed. "Not really. In all the mess that the thieves left behind, I've misplaced my reading glasses. I'm afraid I can't see the print very well."

Jessica sat down and picked up the paper. "I'll be glad to read it to you," she volunteered.

Mrs. Harrington smiled. "Why, that would be wonderful, dear. I'll get our tea. And I've bought some cookies."

For the next twenty minutes, Jessica read to Mrs. Harrington from the local paper, while the two of them sipped their tea and ate cookies. She was almost finished with the news when she spotted an announcement.

"Oh, here's something interesting," she said. "An acting workshop! 'In four Saturday-morning sessions,' " she read, " 'this workshop will enable young performers to study voice, gesture, movement, and various other techniques of stagecraft.' " Jessica wrinkled her nose. "It sounds like a lot of work."

"But acting *is* work," Mrs. Harrington replied. "The body and the voice are the actor's basic tools, and if he doesn't know how to use those tools, all the wishing in the world won't make him—or her—an actor."

"But isn't acting fun, as well as work?" Jessica asked. "Being in the school musical was a lot of fun." Even though she hadn't played the lead role, she had loved every minute of it.

Mrs. Harrington laughed. "I guess it depends on your definition of fun," she said. "I loved being on stage. It was the greatest joy of my life! But I worked very hard, every single minute I was there." She straightened her shoulders and studied Jessica. "Many young people think they have talent," she said firmly, "but not all of them want to put in the work it takes to learn to act. If you really care about acting, Jessica, you should sign up for the workshop. It will give you a taste of what's involved in acting. And you'll very quickly find out whether you have any real talent or not."

Jessica frowned. She knew she had real talent. She knew she wanted to act. But spending four whole Saturdays in a row at a workshop— and an *early* morning workshop, at that—seemed like a very high price to pay. Still, if she said no, Mrs. Harrington might think that she didn't really care about acting.

"Well, all right," Jessica said, trying to sound enthusiastic. "I guess I'll sign up."

Seven

On Tuesday afternoon, Jessica called the number she had cut out from the paper and enrolled in the acting workshop. She still wasn't convinced it was the best idea, since she didn't like hard work, but she didn't want to disappoint Mrs. Harrington.

Over the phone, the workshop director said he would be mailing her a booklet to read about acting—suggestions for speaking and moving and ideas for getting into a character on stage. He suggested that she read the booklet and practice acting out a couple of scenes in front of the mirror before she came to the first workshop.

But by Saturday morning, Jessica hadn't read the booklet or practiced any scenes. In fact, she almost overslept. At eight-fifteen, Elizabeth pounded on her door.

"Jessica! Are you still asleep? Doesn't the workshop start at nine-thirty?"

Jessica pulled the covers over her head. "I don't think I'm going," she muttered sleepily. "I like to sleep late on Saturdays." But then she remembered Mrs. Harrington and how excited she was about the whole thing. Jessica had promised to stop by her house when the workshop was over and tell her all about it. With a big sigh, she dragged herself out of bed, brushed her teeth, got dressed, and hurried off to the workshop.

"I can tell by your face, Jessica," Mrs. Harrington said when she opened the door that afternoon, "that your workshop went well." Jessica noticed that for the first time since the accident,

Mrs. Harrington wasn't wearing her neck brace. "Come in and tell me about it," she invited.

Jessica followed Mrs. Harrington into the kitchen, gesturing excitedly. "I can't believe it was so much fun!" she cried.

"Fun?" Mrs. Harrington teased. "I thought it was going to be nothing but work. What happened to all the technique they were going to teach you?"

"Oh, they are teaching technique," Jessica replied. "But it's the way they teach it that's so much fun. It's like playing games!"

"Why don't you show me what you learned," Mrs. Harrington suggested, setting out teacups and a plate of blueberry muffins.

Jessica stood up. "We did mimes," she said. She bent over and with great care began to wriggle into an invisible ski suit. She fastened the hood and pulled down a pair of goggles over her eyes. Then she carefully put on a pair of invisible boots and skis, dug her ski poles into the deep snow, and got ready to go down an imaginary slope—a very *steep* slope.

"I know!" Mrs. Harrington exclaimed, clapping her hands. "You're a skier! Jessica, that's very good!"

Jessica sat down, flushed with pleasure.

"I especially liked your facial expression at the end," Mrs. Harrington said. "I'm sure I would feel just as horrified as you felt if I were facing a very steep slope."

"I imagined that I was standing at the top of the toughest ski slope at Bear Valley," Jessica confided, "looking down miles and miles of snow."

"That's a wonderful actor's trick," Mrs. Harrington said. "If you have to communicate fear, you can imagine that you're in a frightening situation. And it has to be exaggerated. That way, you're sure to communicate the feeling to your audience." She began to laugh.

"What are you laughing about?" Jessica asked curiously, reaching for a muffin. She had never seen Mrs. Harrington laugh before. It made her look so much younger.

Mrs. Harrington laughed harder. "I'm remembering something funny that happened to me when I was a very young student in New York," she said. "My first acting coach was a tall, graceful Russian woman, Baroness Kraskovitch. I went to her apartment for my lessons. She lived in a very fancy building with a marble foyer and a doorman. She always wore a long black dress, a string of pearls, and a lorgnette—"

"What's a lorgnette?" Jessica interrupted.

"Eyeglasses that are mounted on a long handle," Mrs. Harrington told her. "She used to peer through it at us as if we were bugs under a microscope." She demonstrated, pulling up one shoulder and staring haughtily down her nose. Jessica couldn't help giggling. She could just imagine what the Baroness must have looked like.

"The Baroness," Mrs. Harrington went on, "was extremely dignified, and she almost never smiled. Anyway, my partner and I were doing mimes, just the way you did today, only we were doing animal mimes. We had done dogs and cats and horses, and we were supposed to do chickens next. But living in New York, we had never even *seen* a chicken, so we had no idea how to mime one."

She paused, and Jessica sat forward on the edge of her seat. "And then what happened?"

"Well, we gave it our best effort, of course," Mrs. Harrington said. "But our best clearly wasn't good enough for the Baroness. *'Nyet! Nyet!'* she shouted, slipping into Russian. 'I must *see* this chicken.' She flung down her lorgnette, hitched up her long black skirt, flung her pearls over her shoulder to keep them out of the way, and got down on the floor to show us how to do a chicken."

And with that, Mrs. Harrington herself squatted in the middle of the kitchen floor with her arms tucked back along her sides like wings. Then she began to dart her head quickly from side to side in a perfect imitation of a chicken.

Jessica laughed out loud. In a moment, Mrs. Harrington sat back in her chair, her face flushed and happy.

"I wish you could have seen the Baroness

Kraskovitch being a chicken," Mrs. Harrington said finally. "It was a sight you'd never forget."

Jessica wiped her eyes. "I think I just did."

For the rest of the afternoon, Mrs. Harrington told Jessica stories, each one funnier than the one before, about her days as an acting student in New York. When it was time for Jessica to go home, Mrs. Harrington looked happier, more relaxed, and more beautiful than she had ever seen her.

She asked Jessica to come back during the week to practice the scenes the director had assigned for the following Saturday. Jessica agreed happily. Practicing in front of Mrs. Harrington sounded like a lot more fun than practicing in front of the mirror. Maybe she could even get Mrs. Harrington to give her a few pointers on acting.

As Mrs. Harrington saw Jessica to the door, she picked up a framed picture from the hallway table. "By the way, Jessica," she said, "I found this old picture in one of my drawers this morning. I thought you might like to have it."

Jessica took the picture. It was a studio photo of Dolores Dufay, smiling her famous smile into the camera. At the bottom, in a beautiful, flowing script, it said, "To Jessica Wakefield, who will be a fine actress one day—if she works hard enough! With love, Dolores Dufay."

"Oh, thank you, Mrs. . . . Miss Dufay!" Jessica cried. This picture was a thousand times better than an autograph!

Mrs. Harrington smiled and waved as Jessica went down the sidewalk with her precious picture under her arm. She decided it was definitely time to tell Lila and Ellen about her acting career, and about her new friend and acting coach, the famous Dolores Dufay.

"I don't believe you," Lila announced flatly when Jessica had finished her story at lunchtime on Monday.

"I don't believe you either, Jessica," Ellen said. "I think you're just trying to get out of some Unicorn meetings, that's all."

Jessica shrugged one shoulder, as she had

seen Dolores Dufay do. Then she opened her notebook and pulled out the autographed picture. "Would you believe this?" she asked.

Lila stared at the photograph in awed silence. She blinked and swallowed. "How did you say you met Miss Dufay?" she asked at last.

Jessica gave her a mysterious smile.

"Could *we* meet her?" Ellen inquired.

"Maybe," Jessica said in a teasing voice. "If you'd like to come to the performance at the end of the workshop, that is. Miss Dufay will be there, of course. I'll be glad to introduce you."

Jessica was sure that Mrs. Harrington would say yes to her invitation. And Lila and Ellen would be terribly impressed when they saw Jessica and Miss Dufay together.

Now Lila and Ellen were looking at Jessica with new respect.

"We'll definitely come to your performance," Lila said.

"We wouldn't miss it for anything," Ellen agreed.

Eight

◇

For the next three weeks, Jessica found herself working harder than she had ever worked in her life. For the final performance, the workshop director had assigned each student two scenes to be performed with a partner. Jessica's partner was a shy, slender boy named Martin. Their two scenes made up a very short play for children called *The Kite*. The plot was very simple, so small children could understand it, but it was also very moving. A young girl and boy work hard to build a special kite, shaped like a giant bird. When they fly it for the first time, the boy loses hold of the string and lets the kite fly away. But instead of getting angry and upset about the loss of the kite, the girl explains that it was meant to be free. "Don't you see," she says to the boy, "our kite is like a great bird. And now it's free to fly as high and far as it dares." Jessica especially liked the way the play ended, and she loved having the last lines for herself.

When Jessica showed Mrs. Harrington the script for *The Kite*, the old woman was delighted.

"Why, I've performed in this play dozens of times," she said. "When I was a student, I played the boy, and my best friend Eleanor played the girl." Her voice softened. "And later, I played it with Richard in a dramatic series we did for children."

"Would you like to read the boy's lines?" Jessica asked. "Martin can only practice on Saturday, so it would be a big help if you'd read with me."

"Of course, Jessica." The week after the second workshop, they worked together on the script every afternoon. Finally, Jessica knew her part by heart. And then, because Mrs. Harrington knew the play so well and had performed in it so often, she began giving Jessica advice on how to play the scenes, how to move, how to speak.

Jessica was amazed at the way the lines came to life when Mrs. Harrington delivered them. She may have been away from the stage for many years, but when she was acting, it was as if she had never stopped. When she was playing the part of the twelve-year-old boy, it was impossible to believe that she was a sixty-five-year-old woman. Her voice was light, her step was springy, and her body was straight and strong.

"Why don't you go back to acting again?" Jessica couldn't help asking. "I'm sure there are *lots* of parts you could play."

All of a sudden, Mrs. Harrington was a sixty-five-year-old woman again, her face lined and tired.

"Oh, I couldn't go back," she said, sitting down wearily. "I've been away from the business much too long. Actors don't take a vacation from their work, you know. When you're out of work for a little while, people forget who you are!"

"But nobody could ever forget Dolores Dufay," Jessica protested.

Mrs. Harrington laughed and put her hand on Jessica's shoulder. "Thank you, my dear," she said. "But I'm much too old to start again. And that's the end of that." She stood up. "Back to the play. Let's take it from the top of page three, shall we? There's a rough spot there that we need to iron out."

On the Friday afternoon before the performance, Mrs. Harrington announced that she was very proud of her student and she wanted to see her on stage. She couldn't accept Jessica's invitation to come to the performance on Saturday evening because she didn't go out at night. But she would be glad to come to the dress rehearsal and final workshop on Saturday afternoon.

Jessica didn't know what to do. After all, she had promised Lila and Ellen that she would introduce them to Dolores Dufay. She called them to ask them if they could come to the Saturday afternoon dress rehearsal instead. But as it turned out, they had other plans.

"If you ask me, Jessica," Lila said huffily, "you're just making excuses. I'll bet that Dolores Dufay won't be at the rehearsal, either."

"Yes, she will," Jessica said, feeling defensive. "If you and Ellen will come, you'll meet her."

"Well, we can't come," Lila said. "So we'll see you tomorrow night." Her voice took on a warning edge. "And your performance had better be good, Jessica. After all, you've missed an awful lot of Unicorn meetings over the past few weeks! You'd better have something to show for it."

"Oh, I'll be good," Jessica said smugly. "You just wait and see."

When she put down the phone, Jessica felt disappointed. She had wanted Lila and Ellen to meet Miss Dufay and see for themselves that she was being coached by a famous movie star. But then she decided that maybe things had worked out for the best. After all, Mrs. Harrington didn't exactly *look* like a famous movie star anymore.

Finally it was Saturday, the day of the dress rehearsal and the workshop. Jessica was down in the basement, rummaging frantically through the storage room.

"What are you looking for?" Elizabeth asked, coming down the stairs.

"I'm looking for that old kite of Steven's," Jessica said, taking a box down. "You know, the one that looks like a big gold bird. I promised the director that I'd bring it to the dress rehearsal today. I'd better go and ask Steven if he knows where it is."

She ran upstairs to the kitchen where Steven was finishing up a tall stack of pancakes.

"You need that old kite?" he asked. "Sorry,

too late. I threw it away weeks ago. It was all ripped up."

"You threw it away?" Jessica wailed desperately. "But I need it! We can't do the play without it!"

"So buy another one," Steven said, taking his plate to the sink. "Kites are cheap."

Jessica was near tears. Why hadn't she remembered to look for the kite earlier? "Elizabeth, where am I supposed to find a kite like that?" she asked.

"Well, you could try that funny little kitemaker's stand at the flea market," she said. "I think that's where Steven got it in the first place." She looked at her watch. "I'll come with you, Jess. But we can't take all day. Mischief needs to get her shots, and I'm planning to take her to the vet's this afternoon."

"Oh, this won't take long," Jessica assured her. "Besides, I have to be at rehearsal at one."

The flea market was already crowded by the time Elizabeth and Jessica got there. While Jessica dashed off to find the kite-maker's stand, Elizabeth stopped at a stall and began to look through a pile of old books with ornate leather bindings and gold lettering. The first book she picked up was a collection of Shakespeare plays.

And the next book she picked up took her breath away. The book had fallen open to the title page, and on it was inscribed, in careful script, "To my beloved Dolores, from Richard."

It was one of Mrs. Harrington's books!

At that moment, Jessica came back, carrying a big gold kite shaped like a bird.

"I found it!" she announced happily. "Boy, was that lucky! This was the very last bird kite!"

Putting her finger to her lips, Elizabeth drew her twin aside. "Look," she whispered, opening the book.

Jessica gasped. "It's Mrs. Harrington's book!" she cried. Then she clapped her hand over her mouth, looking around to see whether anyone had heard her. The stall owner was talking to another customer.

"How much money do you have?" Elizabeth

whispered. "We have to buy this book and take it to the police to show them. It's evidence of the burglary!"

Jessica bit her lip. "I spent every last cent on this kite," she said. "How much do you have?"

Elizabeth opened her purse. "Only fifty cents."

"We'll just have to run home and get more money," Jessica said.

"We'd better hurry," Elizabeth said. "It's starting to drizzle. The vendor may leave if it starts to rain hard."

"Let's go, then," Jessica cried.

They raced home, raided their savings, and raced back, wearing their raincoats. But by the time they got back to the flea market, it was pouring. The stall was empty. All the books were gone!

"Now what do we do?" Jessica cried anxiously. "We've got to find that man!"

"Look over there!" Elizabeth pointed. "It's the bookseller! He's putting the books into his van!"

The two girls hurried over to him. "I noticed an old collection of plays a little while ago,"

Jessica said breathlessly. "Do you suppose I could see it again?"

"Can't you see I've already packed everything up? How am I supposed to find it?"

"Oh, please," Jessica begged. "If you let me look through a couple of boxes I'm sure I'll recognize it right away."

The vendor grunted angrily, but he removed a couple of boxes. While Jessica looked for the book, Elizabeth ran around to the front of the van and wrote down the license plate number. When she got back, Jessica was just handing the vendor four dollars for Mrs. Harrington's book.

As soon as they left the flea market, the two girls hurried to the police station. They found Officer Carey behind his desk, looking over some paperwork.

"Look what we found!" Jessica announced triumphantly, laying the book of old plays open on the desk in front of him.

Officer Carey whistled when he saw the inscription. "Where did you girls get this?" he demanded.

Elizabeth pulled out the license plate number. "From the man who drives this van. It's a white Ford."

Officer Carey stood up and pushed back his chair. "I'll get on this right away. Congratulations, girls. You might have found our burglar!"

Nine

◇

Jessica arrived at the final workshop at exactly one o'clock. Everybody was gathered in the dressing rooms backstage, putting makeup on and getting ready for the dress rehearsal. She quickly slipped onto a stool in front of a mirror and put on some dark pink lipstick.

"Hello, Jessica," a voice said behind her. Jessica turned around and saw Mrs. Harrington. She was wearing a silk dress and she had swept her white hair up on top of her head in a loose bun. She looked very nice, but Jessica still didn't think that anybody would guess who she was.

"Hi, Mrs. Harrington," Jessica said excitedly. "I'm so glad you could come!"

For a moment, she thought of telling Mrs. Harrington that Elizabeth had discovered her book in the flea market and the police were looking for the thief right now. But then she thought that maybe the police wouldn't find anything. It probably wasn't a good idea to get Mrs. Harrington's hopes up until they had some really positive news to tell her.

"I'm glad I came, too," Mrs. Harrington whispered, glancing from the costume racks to the makeup tables. "It's been a very long time since I was backstage before a performance. It brings back so many memories." She smiled. "I'd forgotten what a warm, wonderful sense of anticipation everybody feels just before a performance. It always made me tingly inside."

Jessica laughed. "I thought that tingle was just a bad case of nerves."

Mrs. Harrington nodded. "Those, too," she

replied. "I don't think I ever put on a performance when I wasn't absolutely petrified for the first three minutes." Her lips curved up in a soft smile. "But after that, I just seemed to forget that the audience was there. And the nerves disappeared. I'm sure the same thing will happen for you, too."

Jessica took Mrs. Harrington's hand. "Let me introduce you to some of my friends in the workshop. Everybody will be so excited when they find out there's a real actress in the audience."

Mrs. Harrington took a step back. "Oh, no," she said, shaking her head firmly. "I don't want anyone to make a fuss. I'd rather just look around a little. When the time comes for your performance, I'll be in the front row watching, dear." She smiled and touched Jessica's cheek with her finger. "Break a leg, Jessica."

Jessica looked startled.

"It's an actor's way of wishing you good luck," Mrs. Harrington told her. "Richard and I always said it to each other before our performances."

Jessica grinned. "Thanks," she said. "I need all the luck I can get."

For the next few moments, while Jessica finished putting on her makeup, Mrs. Harrington wandered around backstage, looking at the props and fingering the costumes. Then she went out to the darkened auditorium and sat down in the front row.

After the first two pairs of performers were finished with their scenes, Elizabeth came into the theater and sat down in the front row beside her. Carefully, she placed a covered picnic basket on the floor between them.

"Hello, Mrs. Harrington," Elizabeth whispered. "Have Jessica and Martin done their scenes yet?" she asked. She was supposed to meet Jessica after the rehearsal so they could stop back at the police station and talk to Officer Carey. They hoped that he might have some new information about the robbery.

"Hello, Elizabeth," Mrs. Harrington said warmly. "Your sister is next, I think." On the floor, the basket between them began to rock and bounce. Curiously, she looked down at it. "What do you have in your basket?"

Elizabeth laughed. "Want to see?" she asked. She opened the basket lid and lifted Mischief out. "I just took her to the vet's to get her shots."

Mrs. Harrington smiled and stroked the white spot under Mischief's chin. "She looks just like a kitten I had once, when I was about your age. She slept with me at night and spent the day out on our fire escape, watching the birds. I used to love to listen to her purr on the pillow beside me as I was falling asleep." She smiled as Mischief leaped into her lap and began to pat the black beads that hung around her neck.

Remembering how upset Mrs. Harrington had been when the puppy jumped all over everything, Elizabeth picked Mischief up and tried to put her back into the basket. 'I'm sorry," she said. "I hope she didn't hurt your dress. Now, Mischief," she told the kitten, "be good and stay in your basket until the play's over."

But Mischief had other ideas. Without an instant's hesitation, she jumped out of the basket and right back onto Mrs. Harrington's lap. Mrs. Harrington put her hand over the kitten.

"She's all right where she is, Elizabeth," she said, stroking Mischief's soft fur. "In fact, I think she's going to sleep."

"Oh, look. Here's Jessica," Elizabeth announced.

Jessica and Martin walked out to the center of the stage. When they started performing their scene, Martin seemed very nervous and unsure of himself, and several times he flubbed his lines. Once he left out an entire speech. But Jessica knew the play so well that she was able to cover up for him, and the performance went pretty smoothly.

When they were finished, the director, who was sitting at the other end of the front row, stood up and applauded.

"Wonderful!" he exclaimed. "If you two do as well tonight you'll be real stars. Jessica, your timing was great, and your last lines were perfect. Martin, maybe you'd better run through your lines a few more times before this evening. Try to relax a little, OK?"

On stage, Jessica beamed. She waved down at Elizabeth and Mrs. Harrington and blew them both a kiss before she disappeared into the wings.

Mrs. Harrington applauded, too. She handed Mischief back to Elizabeth and stood up. "Your sister is very talented."

Elizabeth nodded. She could see from the easy, confident way that Jessica handled herself on stage that Mrs. Harrington was right. Her twin had a flair for acting.

"Of course," Mrs. Harrington continued, "having talent doesn't mean that Jessica will become an actress. Lots of people with talent don't have the day-to-day discipline that's required for a life on the stage or in front of the camera. It's not an easy life."

Elizabeth remembered how hard it had been for Jessica to wake up on the Saturday morning of the first workshop. But she *had* gotten up, and she had worked very hard for the last few weeks.

"It takes more than just hard work," Mrs. Harrington continued. "One also needs support from people who care, and a lot of good luck." She smiled. "I was very fortunate. I had all three."

They walked out of the auditorium together and then waited for Jessica to join them. "Don't you ever miss being on stage?" Elizabeth asked. "After a whole lifetime in the theater, giving it up must have been very hard."

"You know, it's interesting," Mrs. Harrington said. "If you had asked me that a month or so ago, I would have said no. It wasn't hard at all. Without Richard, a life in the theater didn't seem worth living. Oh, every once in a while, maybe, I'd think about it. But for the past few weeks, since I've been working with your sister, I've thought about it more often. And today, when I went backstage—" She stopped and laughed a little, sadly. "Today, for the first time, I started to think perhaps it was a mistake to give it up."

At that moment, Jessica came up, still wearing her makeup. "Well," she demanded excitedly, "what did you think?"

Mrs. Harrington looked at Jessica with a warm glow in her eyes. "Jessica, my dear," she said, "you were absolutely wonderful!"

"I was?" she asked breathlessly. "Did you think so, too, Elizabeth?"

Elizabeth laughed. "Yes," she said, "I thought so, too. Especially when you were able to help Martin without calling attention to the fact that he'd messed up his lines."

"That's the mark of a fine actor, Jessica," Mrs. Harrington said. "Not only do you know your own part very well, but you know all the parts. In an emergency, you can cover for the others."

Jessica looked pleased. "I wish you could come tonight," she said. "I think the play will be even better when we have to give it in front of a real audience. Well," she added worriedly, "as long as Martin doesn't blow his lines again. He's got a bad case of stage fright."

"I'm sure you'll be fine tonight, Jessica." Mrs. Harrington turned to Elizabeth "Thank you for introducing me to Mischief," she said. She tipped up the lid of the picnic basket and stroked Mischief's head with one finger.

Mischief purred loudly and Elizabeth smiled.

"Hey, Elizabeth," Jessica cried. "I almost forgot. Don't we have an errand to run? We'd better be going."

Elizabeth nodded. They said goodbye to Mrs. Harrington and raced off to the police station to talk to Officer Carey.

Ten

◇

"You two cracked the case," Officer Carey announced when Jessica and Elizabeth arrived at his office.

"We did?" Elizabeth squeaked.

"Really?" Jessica asked excitedly.

Officer Carey nodded and pointed to a big box in the corner. "We checked the license plate, got an address and a warrant, and searched the vendor's house. Not only did we find most of Mrs. Harrington's missing items—including that scrapbook you were looking for—but the vendor confessed to several burglaries. So he's spending the evening behind bars."

But Jessica wasn't interested in the burglar. "You found the scrapbook?" she cried out.

"We sure did." Officer Carey grinned.

"Could we see it?" Jessica asked.

"Sure," the policeman replied. He took it out of the box in the corner, and handed it to Jessica. "We'll return everything to Mrs. Harrington tomorrow," Officer Carey said.

Jessica leafed through the scrapbook. "She'll be so glad to have this back. Would you mind if we took the scrapbook with us, Officer Carey? We'd like to return it to Mrs. Harrington ourselves."

"I don't see any problem with that. After all, if it weren't for you two, we might never have found it," he said. "You'll just have to sign for it." He filled out a slip and they signed it.

"Thanks again, girls. You two will make great detectives some day."

Jessica and Elizabeth smiled and said goodbye.

"When do you think we ought to give the

scrapbook to Mrs. Harrington?" Jessica asked as they walked home.

"How about tonight, after the performance?" Elizabeth suggested. "I'll bet Mom and Dad would be glad to take us there." She smiled, thinking about how happy Mrs. Harrington had looked this afternoon, holding Mischief, watching Jessica. Then suddenly, she had an idea—an idea so right she was amazed she hadn't thought of it earlier. Tonight, when they took the scrapbook to Mrs. Harrington, they could take her another present, too.

Just as they walked in the door of their house, the telephone rang. Jessica picked it up as Elizabeth let Mischief out of her basket.

"Hello," Jessica said. She listened for a minute, then grinned and jumped up and down. "Yes, Mrs. Harrington," she said excitedly, "that'll be wonderful! Great! We'll see you at the auditorium tonight!"

Elizabeth understood. Mrs. Harrington must have changed her mind and decided to come tonight.

"Invite her to come over here after the performance," she said. "I'm sure Mom and Dad won't mind."

Jessica nodded. "Elizabeth and I were wondering if you'd like to come back to our house after the performance." Mrs. Harrington must have said yes, because Jessica smiled again. "That's great! We'll see you tonight." She hung up.

"Wonderful!" Elizabeth exclaimed, dancing around in a circle. "We can have ice cream, then you can give her the scrapbook. Won't she be surprised?" *And I can give her my present, too*, she thought to herself.

Jessica picked up the phone and began to dial.

"Who are you calling now?" Elizabeth asked.

"Lila and Ellen," Jessica said. "I've got to tell them that Dolores Dufay will be at the performance tonight, after all. Maybe they'd like to bring some of the other Unicorns." She stopped dialing. "Oh, and Lizzie, don't forget your camera. I'd really love it if you could get a picture of

Miss Dufay and me together after the performance. That would make the Unicorns turn absolutely green with envy." She turned back to the phone. "Hi, Lila, it's Jessica," she said. "Guess what?"

Elizabeth grinned and shook her head. Jessica would never change.

With only fifteen minutes to go before the performance, Jessica was backstage, nervously going over her lines one more time. Once she had put on her makeup, she didn't have anything else to do but sit around and feel anxious. She went to the blue velvet curtain that was pulled across the stage and peeked out. The house lights were still on, and she could see that the auditorium was almost full.

She spotted her family in the second row, all dressed up. Elizabeth's blond hair was pulled back in a sleek ponytail, and she was wearing her new blue dress. Her mother was wearing a very pretty white suit. Next to her sat Steven, uncomfortable and fidgety in his sports jacket.

And beside Steven was her handsome father. And beside him—

Jessica blinked. Beside her father was Dolores Dufay! She rubbed her eyes and looked again. Yes, there was absolutely no doubt of it. Mrs. Harrington had become Dolores Dufay once again! She had put on makeup and styled her white hair in a beautifully graceful and attractive way, so that she looked at least ten years younger. She was wearing an elegant dark suit with an ivory silk blouse, a long string of pearls, and a pair of dangly pearl earrings. Every now and then, when Jessica's father said something to her, she would give him the famous Dufay smile.

Jessica could hardly believe it. Old Mrs. Harrington had disappeared, and in her place was a beautiful, glamorous movie star. She scanned the audience, hoping that Lila and Ellen were there. They would recognize Dolores Dufay, especially when they saw her sitting with the Wakefields.

Jessica smiled blissfully. What a wonderful evening it was going to be! She could imagine it all—the thunderous applause when she delivered her last lines, Miss Dufay hurrying up to kiss her and tell her what a fabulous job she had done, and best of all, the looks on Lila's and Ellen's faces when she introduced them to the glamorous movie star. It was all too good to be true!

"There you are, Jessica," the director said anxiously. "I've been looking for you everywhere!"

Jessica turned around and dropped the corner of the curtain. "Is it time?" she asked nervously.

The director put his arm around her shoulders. "I'm very sorry to tell you this," he began.

"What?" Jessica asked. "What's wrong?"

The director cleared his throat. "Martin has a terrible case of stage fright."

"Oh," Jessica said, relieved, "is that all?" Martin had been scared this afternoon, too, and he'd done all right.

"Where is he? Maybe I can make him feel better."

The director shook his head. "No, Jessica. He

didn't show up tonight. He just called to tell me he won't be coming."

Jessica stared at him. "He's not coming?"

"I'm sorry, Jessica. Without Martin, you won't be able to perform."

Elizabeth leaned forward in her seat. "You mean," she breathed in horror, "that you won't get to do your play?"

Jessica's blue-green eyes were brimming with tears. She nodded. "The director's going to cancel my scenes."

"Oh, Jessica," Mrs. Wakefield said, "that's too bad!"

"I got dressed up for nothing," Steven grumbled.

At the end of the row, Mrs. Harrington stood up. "No, you didn't," she said firmly. She held out her hand. "Come on, Jessica."

Jessica gave her a bewildered look. "Come where?"

"Why, to the dressing room! I'm sure we can

find some men's clothes to fit me. And I have to put on makeup."

Jessica blinked. "You'll do the play with me?"

"You *bet*," Mrs. Harrington said. "Let's hurry!"

Twenty minutes later, the audience in the Sweet Valley Community Theater was treated to an unforgettable performance of *The Kite*, starring Jessica Wakefield and the beautiful, glamorous Dolores Dufay—dressed up in men's clothes, with an old hat crammed down over her white hair. With the actress beside her on the stage, Jessica performed her role better than she had in any of the rehearsals. She delivered her final lines powerfully and the audience exploded into applause. It was a wonderful, thrilling moment, a moment Jessica would never forget.

Eleven

◇

Back at the Wakefields' house, Mrs. Harrington put down her dish of ice cream and looked around at the family. "I can't begin to tell you," she said warmly, "how much Jessica—and Elizabeth, too—have meant to me in the past few weeks. In fact, I think Jessica is responsible for my decision."

"What decision?" Elizabeth asked.

Mrs. Harrington smiled. "I'm going back to acting. On Monday, I'll get in touch with my old agent. I'm very excited about it. Thank you,

Jessica, for reminding me how much I love acting!"

Jessica jumped up and gave Mrs. Harrington a hug. "That's wonderful news! And now, we've got a present for you," she said. "Come on, Elizabeth."

"No, we have *two* presents," Elizabeth corrected her.

Together, Jessica and Elizabeth brought out the scrapbook, which they had carefully gift-wrapped. When Mrs. Harrington opened it, tears came to her eyes. "All my precious memories! You've given them back to me again!"

When the girls told the story of how the scrapbook had been retrieved, everybody was amazed, including Steven. As Elizabeth watched Mrs. Harrington smiling the famous Dufay smile through her tears, she felt very proud.

At that moment, Mischief appeared and jumped right into Mrs. Harrington's lap.

"That's the other present we have for you," Elizabeth said, pointing to Mischief. "I think she likes you better than anyone."

Mrs. Harrington looked surprised. "That's very sweet of you, dear. But won't you miss her?"

"I can always come and visit her at your house," Elizabeth said. "I have this feeling she'd be happier with you." She looked at Jessica and smiled. She knew her twin wouldn't mind seeing Mischief go. And it would be nice for Mrs. Harrington to have someone to keep her company all the time.

"Well, thank you, girls. Both of you are welcome at my house any time. And bring your friends, too."

Jessica grinned widely. She couldn't wait to take Ellen and Lila to visit the famous Dolores Dufay! Maybe she'd even bring Janet Howell, the president of the Unicorn Club.

Now that the workshop was over, she would certainly be spending more time with the Unicorns, and she had to do something to make up for all her missed meetings. Acting had been fun, but as usual, Jessica felt ready to move on to something new.

On Monday morning, Jessica was surrounded

by fellow classmates who had heard about her triumph on Saturday night.

"Are you going to be in a movie with Dolores Dufay?" Sandra Ferris asked.

"I heard you're going to New York to perform your play on Broadway, Jessica," said Ken Matthews.

Jessica loved the attention and didn't bother to explain that what her classmates were saying wasn't true. And she wasn't about to tell them she was considering giving up acting. She wondered who was responsible for starting the rumors when she saw Caroline Pearce, the sixth-grade gossip, approaching in the hall. She probably had started a few of them.

But when Caroline had everyone's attention, instead of congratulating Jessica or asking when she was moving to Hollywood, she announced, "Have you heard? It's really true. Ten members of the East German boys' gymnastics team are coming to Sweet Valley and the best one on the team is staying at *my* house!"

Everyone started talking at once and Jessica

no longer had the spotlight. Now all eyes were turned on Caroline.

"They're arriving at the end of next week," Caroline continued in a loud voice. "The one staying with me is *incredibly* handsome."

Jessica and Elizabeth broke away from the crowd. "I feel sorry for whoever has to stay with her," Jessica said.

"Oh, Jess," Elizabeth said. "Don't be so sour. Just because everyone stopped paying attention to you when Caroline made her announcement . . . Anyway, it'll be great. I can't wait to meet the team. And don't forget, they're all *boys*. Aren't you excited about having ten new boys at school?"

*What will the East German boys be like? Find out in Sweet Valley Twins #33, **THE WAKEFIELDS' VISITOR.***